This EXTREMELY
very good
BOOK belongs to

....

Text based on scripts written by Bridget Hurst and Carol Noble, and Dave Ingham. Samantha Hill and Dave Ingham. Illustrations from the TV animation produced by Tiger Aspect

PUFFIN BOOKS
Published by the Penguin Group; London, New York,
Australia, Canada, India, Ireland, New Zealand and South Africa
Penguin Books Ltd, Registered Offices: 80 Strand, London WC2R 0RL, England

puffinbooks.com

We Honestly Can Look After Your Dog first published in 2005
Whoops! But It Wasn't Me first published in 2006
My Wobbly Tooth Must Not Ever Never Fall Out first published in 2006
I've Won, No I've Won, No I've Won first published in 2005
Snow Is My Favourite and My Best first published in 2006

Published in this edition 2008
007-10 9 8 7

characters created by

lauren child

My
COMPLETELY
best **story**
collection

Contents

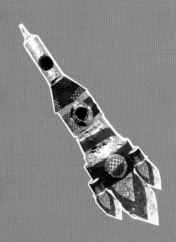

My
wobbly tooth
must not ever
NEVER fall out

I've won, NO I'VE WON, No I've won

Snow is
my FAVOURITE
and my
best

We
honestly
CAN look after
your dog

I have this little sister Lola.
She is small and very funny.
At the moment Lola really, really wants to have a dog.
But Mum and Dad say she can't because our flat
is too small and Lola is too young to look after one.

Lola says,
"Say **woof**, Charlie."

So I say,
"Woof."

Then Lola says, "**Sit!**"

So I sit.

My
cereal
bowl

is

now

a **dog** bowl.

And she has made me a dog bed.

Lola just loves dogs.

A lot.

One day Dad took us to the park.

There was me and my friend Marv,
Lola and her friend Lotta.
And Sizzles.
Sizzles is Marv's dog.

Lola loves Sizzles.

So does Lola's best friend, Lotta.

Lola says, "You ask."
Lotta says, "No you ask."

So Lola says,
"Marv, can we look after Sizzles?"

Marv says,
"Lola, do you know
about dogs?"

Lola says,
"Yes I do. Everything."

And Lotta says, "So do I."

Lola says,

"We know that Sizzles is a very extremely very clever dog. We know he can do very good tricks."

Lotta says, "If he wanted he could roll over."

Lola says,
"And **dance.**
Definitely, I think.
Lotta, do you know
I think
Sizzles
can do
really
anything."

Lola says,
"And
walk
on
two
legs."

Lotta says,
"And **speak English.**"

While Marv is trying to
make Sizzles sit, I see some of our
friends playing football
and I think I'd really like to play too.

So I say,
"We could play just one game,
Marv?"

Marv says,
"But who is going to look after
Sizzles?"

Lola says, "**Me!**"

Lotta says, "**Me!**"

I say,
"It is only for a little while.
He'll be OK with Lola and Lotta.
I'm pretty sure he will."

So Marv says,
"OK.
But you do know that
there are lots of rules
if you want to
look after Sizzles.

No chocolates.

Or cakes.

And
no sweets
of any kind.

Completely no digging...

and

no chasing birds.

And

no splashing in puddles.

And
NO
taking him
off the
lead."

Marv says,
     "Do you honestly promise to
look after my dog?"

          Lola says, "Honestly,
     we do promise honestly,
               to look after your dog."

     Lotta says,
     "Honestly and promisedly, we do."

Lola says,
"Dogs must be stroked and patted."

Lotta says,
"To tell them we're their friend."

Lola says,
"Playing... is
    what makes dogs happy."

Lotta says,
"And grooming makes dogs feel pretty."

Lola says,
    "Dogs must go outside
and must walk."

Lotta says,
    "Otherwise what is the point
of their legs?"

Then Lola says,
"Lotta, I don't think you really know
all about dogs like me."

And Lotta says,
"Lola, I really do know
everything about dogs."

Lola says, "But Lotta, I'm in charge."

And Lotta says,
"So am I."

Lola says,

"We're both in charge, but I think I was a little bit more in charge than you. that Mary said that I said

You see, Lotta, you must hold the lead like this. See?" Lotta says, "Oh no, Lola. You really must do it like this."

"Oh no!"

"Sizzles, where are you?"

"Where are you, Sizzles?"

"Sizzles,
where
are
you?"

Lola says,
    "Do you think we have
lost him forever?"

        Lotta says,
    "I think he was sad actually."

                Then Lola says...

"Sizzles!"

But then Lola says,
    "Oh no! There are two Sizzleses!"

And Lotta says,
        "No, Lola, there are two dogs.
    But only one is Sizzles."

Lola says,
"But which one?"

Lotta says,
"I don't know."

Lola says,
"The clever one!
Sizzles can do anything, remember?"

Lotta says, "Yes. **Sizzles** can do **anything**...

... **Sizzles** can sit!

Sizzles! Sit. Sit. Sit!"

And Lola says,
"Sit. Sit. Please sit!"

Lotta says,
"Sit, sit, sit.
Will you sit!"

Then Lola says,
"Sizzles! It's Sizzles!"

When me and Marv finished playing football,
we went to find Lola and Lotta.
I say, "Come on, you two. It's time to go."

But Lola and Lotta look a bit fidgety.

And they both whisper,
"Charlie, we had Sizzles
and we were
looking after him...

then he sort of went for a walk...

without his lead.
And then we couldn't see him any more.
And then we saw him but he wasn't one,
he was two Sizzleses.

And so... I'm not sure

that Sizzles
is
Sizzles now."

So I say, "Look here! Dog number: 144. Sizzles.
Owner: Marv Lowe,
5a Crocodile Street."

Then Marv says,
"That's his dog tag. It's got his name and address on it,
in case he gets lost.

All dogs have them."

And Lola says,
    "We knew that actually, Marv."

And Lotta says,
    "Just in case
they get lost."

I say,
"Yes, that's right.
    Just in case
they get
    lost!"

And Lola says, "But Sizzles would never get lost."
Lotta says, "Because he's very clever."
Lola says, "He can do absolutely anything."
And Marv says, "Come on, Sizzles, we're going home."

whoOps!
But it wasn't
me

I have this little sister Lola.
She is small and very funny.
Sometimes Lola likes to play
with my things.
Usually I don't mind.

One day I come home from school
    with the best thing I have ever made.

    Lola says, "Ooooh!"

I say,
"It took me ten days,
    three hours and forty minutes
to make the outside,
        which is called
the superstructure...

"... It's built from three cereal packets,

ten yoghurt pots,

28 bottle tops,

157 sweet wrappers and a roll of extra-wide tinfoil."

Lola says, "Ooooh!"

I say, "Don't touch it!
This rocket is really breakable.
I don't mind you playing with
most of my things,
but you must double,
triple promise
you'll NEVER play
with it."

"Let's play something
            else then," says Lola.
      I say, "I've promised to play football
            with Marv."
"But what am I going to do?" says Lola.
            And I say, "Why don't you play
      with Soren Lorensen?"

Soren Lorensen is Lola's imaginary friend.
No one can see him except for Lola.

And Lola says,
      "Soren Lorensen always wants
to play with me."

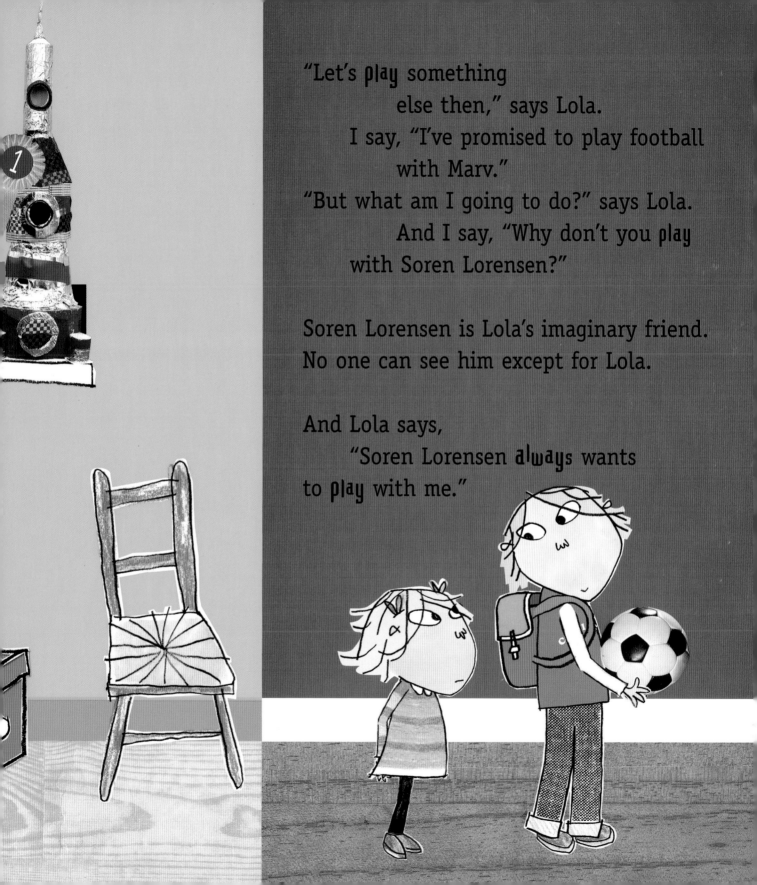

"Hello, Soren Lorensen," says Lola.
"Charlie's gone to play football with Marv,
so we can play a very good game,
can't we?"

And Soren Lorensen says,
        "Yes, with those two hyenas
that are brothers and twins and
        that tiny small elephant."

Lola says, "Oh yes, Ellie.

"Where will the adventure be?"

Soren Lorensen says,
"The place where all the **animals** live."

And Lola says,
"In **Animal** Land."

Soren Lorensen says, "Ellie is really sad because he doesn't like the nasty hyenas laughing at him."

"Those hyenas are meanies, aren't they?" says Lola.
"What are we going to do?"

"We can't leave Ellie all sad," says Lola.
"He must go back to all his nice friends in Animal Land...
but how are we going to get him there?"

Then Soren Lorensen points to the rocket.

Lola says,
"But that is an extremely breakable and special rocket
and Charlie said that we should never,
NEVER touch it or play with it."

"But I think what Charlie meant was that if
we did play with it, we must be extra
specially careful," says Soren Lorensen.

So Lola reaches up to get the rocket.

Soren Lorensen says,
    "Remember to be extra
specially careful, Lola."

And Lola says,

"I am!
I am!"

Then she says,

"Oh no!"

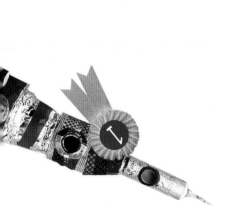

Lola looks at the pieces of broken rocket.
"You know, I think that when
things are broken they can always be
mended and made like new..."

"If we both act normally, Lola,
then Charlie might not think
we did it," says Soren Lorensen.

Lola whispers,
"No, he'll never know."

When I get home I shout,
"My rocket!
Lola!
Did you break
my rocket?"

Lola says,
"I didn't break your
rocket, Charlie."

I say,
"You are telling a big lie, Lola!
And you know it!"

"Don't tell Mum!"
says Lola. "Wait, Charlie!
I just have to quickly talk
to Soren Lorensen."

Lola says, "Do you think we should tell him
what really happened?"
Soren Lorensen says, "Maybe we could tell Charlie
somebody else broke the rocket?"
And Lola says, "Yes! Because it is nearly true!"

So Lola comes to talk to me.
"Charlie, Soren Lorensen and me have got something
very **extremely** important to tell you."

I say, "What?"

Lola says,
"It is the real **true** story of who **broke**
your special **rocket**.

"Well, me and Soren Lorensen were
playing in our room, Charlie,
and Ellie needed to go
in your rocket.

I didn't think it
was a good idea,
but he had to get away.

So we squeezed
Ellie, and it was
a real squish.
But we did it.

And then we took off.

Whoosh! Whoosh!

"... and then
we landed

and
we
were
so
squished
that...

the
rocket
just fell
to
pieces.
And that's
what happened."

I say,

"Right.
I'm going to
tell Mum!"

"Oh dear, I don't think he believed us," says Soren Lorensen.

Lola says,
"I think I have to tell
     Charlie the truth. But will it
make Charlie like me again?"

Soren Lorensen says,
"As long as you say sorry too."

Lola knocks at the door.
"Soren Lorensen
really wants to say **sorry**
for **breaking** your
rocket, Charlie."

So I just shut
the door.

Then there's another knock
and Lola says,
    "It was me that broke
your rocket. Just as I was
    getting your extremely
special rocket down from
the really high shelf...
        it fell and broke
    into lots
            of pieces.

I am really ever so sorry
    for breaking your
extremely special rocket,
        Charlie."

And I say,
"Are you **really**, Lola?"

Lola says, "**Sorry**, Charlie."

And she does look really very sorry.

So I say, "That's OK.
At least you've told the truth."

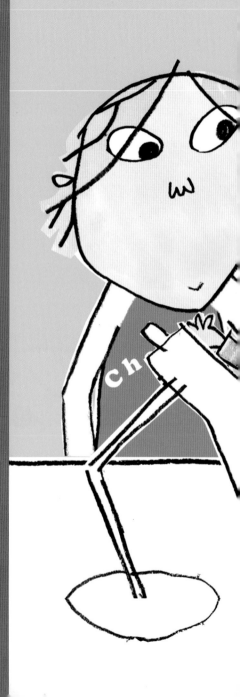
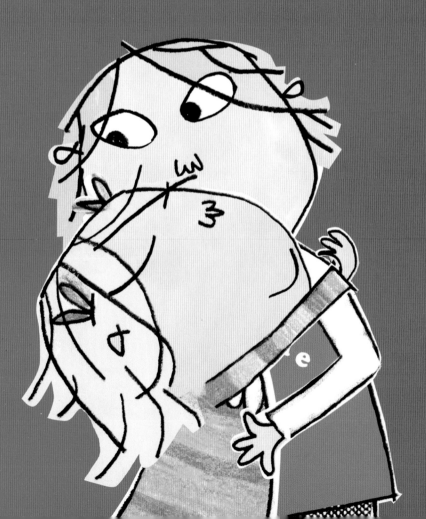

Then Lola sees the rocket.

"You **mend**ed it, Charlie!" she says.

And I say,
"Yes, Lola, I've mended it."

"I like it," says Lola.
I say,
"Don't touch it!"

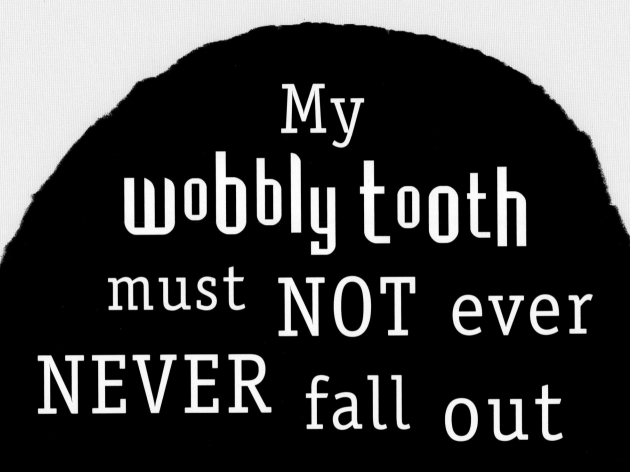

I have this little sister Lola.
She is small and very funny.
This week she got her
first ever wobbly tooth.

Lola says,
"I do not ever NEVER want
my wobbly tooth to fall out."

Marv says, "When I had my first wobbly tooth,
I nearly swallowed it.
Luckily I was eating a toffee...
and my tooth got stuck in it!"

I say, "Once I headed a football
and my **wobbly tooth** just flew out
of my mouth!"

"But I do not ever NEVER
want my **wobbly tooth**
to **fall out**," says Lola.

Marv says, "Why don't
you want it to fall out?"

"I just need to keep completely
all my teeth," says Lola.

And I say, "Those are just your baby teeth
and they are meant to
get wobbly and fall out.
Then you will get new teeth – and
they are your grown-up ones."

"It's like mooses," I say. "Mooses' antlers
fall off and then they get new ones which are
better and stronger."

"But I am not a moose!
It's my wobbly tooth and
I want to keep it... wobbly," says Lola.

Later Lotta comes over to play with Lola.
    "Lola, Lola!"

Lola says,
"What is it, Lotta? What is it?"
And Lotta says,
    "My tooth fell out!"

"What do you **mean**, what did you **get**?" says Lola.
And Lotta says,
"Well, the tooth fairy came and..."
"Who is the tooth fairy?!" says Lola.

"The tooth fairy is the tooth fairy...
    I lost my wobbly tooth, I put it under my pillow,
  and then in the middle of the night
the tooth fairy came and then I got
    a coin," says Lotta.
    "And in the morning
I bought this for
    the farm.
It's a
    chicken!"

Lola says,

"I didn't know there was a special fairy
who gives you presents when your teeth fall out!
Why didn't somebody tell me this before?

"My wobbly tooth must completely
    come out! Now!"

Lotta says,
    "When your tooth falls out,
what are you going to get?
    We need a horse and a sheep...
and a cow."

    And Lola says,
        "I'm going to get
            a giraffe."

"Do you get **giraffes** on a **farm**?"
says Lotta.

And Lola says,
"Yes, you **absolutely** do, Lotta...

"... but how do I get my wobbly tooth to fall out?"

And Lotta says, "Does it feel wobbly enough?"

Lola says, "I think it's almost nearly
about to come out..."
And Lotta says,
"You have to keep wobbling it."

Marv says,
"Do you want me to twist it?"
"No, Marv!" says Lola. "Mum said
absolutely no twisting!"
And I say, "Keep wobbling, Lola."

"I've been **wobbling** it for ages," she says. "It's still not coming **out**.

I don't think it's **ever** going to **come out**."

Then she squeals,
"Aaagh!

It's out!
My wobbly tooth
is really out!
And now I can get my giraffe!"

Lotta says,
   "You have to put it under your pillow
in the very, very middle.
      You must go to bed early,
         and you must fall asleep quickly,
or the tooth fairy won't come."

   Lola says, "Yes. Because I really want
                  my giraffe."

"I want the giraffe too!" says Lotta.

"When you come over tomorrow,"
    says Lola, "I can have my giraffe
and you can bring your chicken
        and they can be friends."

"Yes, yes, yes!" says Lotta.
    "Bye, Lola!"

At bedtime Lola says,
    "Charlie, I'm just going to wash
my **tooth** and make it **shiny** and **clean**.
        And then I...

Oh no!
My tooth has gone!
It's NOT there!"

I say,
    "Check again.
It must be there!"

But Lola says,
"My tooth is
        completely
GONE!"

I say,
"It must be somewhere!"

So we
start
searching
everywhere.

We look in the sink,

and

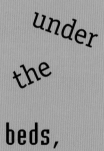

under
the
beds,

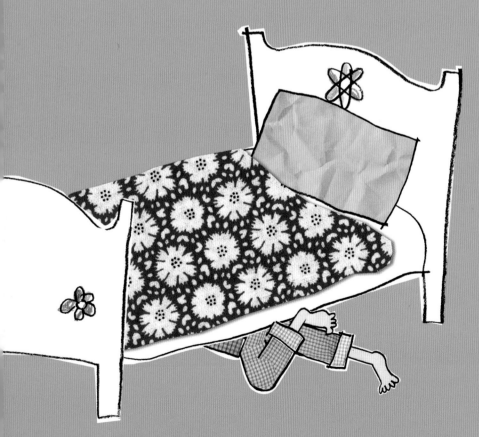

on the floor,

and

around the sofa.

Everywhere.

Then I have a really good idea.

"If you go to sleep and dream really
happy dreams, you will smile.
And then the tooth fairy will see
the gap in your teeth,
and she'll know you really did
lose your tooth!"

So Lola goes to bed.

"Really happy dreams.

Really happy dreams. Really happy..."

In the morning
Lola looks under the very
middle of her pillow.

She says,

"Charlie! The tooth fairy did come!
Look! Hurry, hurry, Charlie,
I need to get a giraffe!"

When Lotta comes to play with Lola she says,
    "What's your **giraffe** called?"
Lola says, "**Giraffe**. And what about your **chicken**?"
    Lotta says, "It's called **Chicken**!"
"Oh **look!** I think they're **friends**," says Lola.

Then Lola says, "Maybe **Giraffe** and **Chicken**
would like to meet Mr **Goat**?
Oh, we don't have a **goat**."
"How will we get a **goat**?" says Lotta.
"We need more **wobbly teeth!**" says Lola.
"Have you got any more **wobbly teeth**?"

Lotta says, "No."
"What about this one?" says Lola.
"No," says Lotta.
Lola says, "Try that one.
This one? This one? This one..."

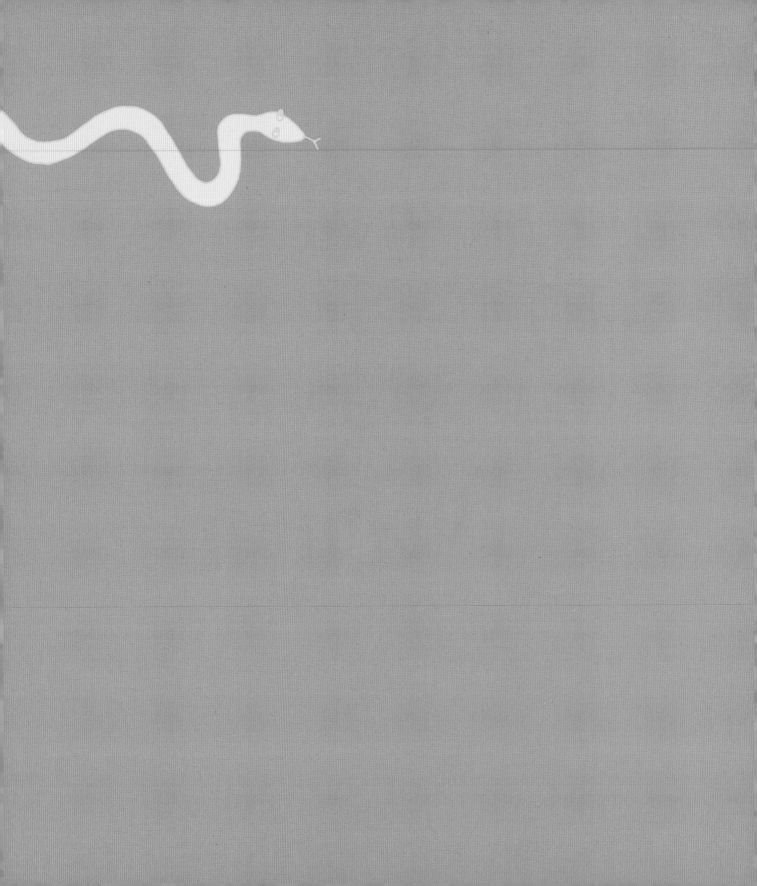

I have this little sister Lola.
She is small and very funny.
When we play "Who can sit
still the longest!"
Lola **always** has to win.

Last time we played, Lola said, "I've won!"

I say,
"But I didn't move!"

Lola says,
"Yes you did! I've won!
I always win...
always,
always,
always!"

And then she says,

"I can run faster than a speedy, speedy cheetah,

and
I
can
stand
on
one leg
longer
than a
flamingo!

And I can bounce higher than a bouncy kangaroo, Charlie! See!"

Even when we're drinking pink milk,
            Lola has to finish first.
      I say,
      "But do you have to win at everything, Lola?"

            And Lola says,

                  "Yep. I've won!"

So I say,
"How about a game
of spoons?"

I know I'm
better than Lola
at the spoon game.

But even so,
Lola says, "I'm winning!"
    I say, "No you're not!"
She says, "I am."
I say, "Not!"

And then Lola
says,
    "Aah, Charlie,
what's that?"

I look up at
    the ceiling
and then when
I look back
    at Lola...

her spoon has **definitely** moved!
    I say,
"Lola, have you... **cheated?**"
    But Lola says,
        "Charlie, I've won!"

So then I say,
"Lola, you remember how to play snap,
don't you?
You need two cards that look the same,
then it's a snap."

Lola says,
"Yes, two cards that look
exactly the same,
then it's a
snap."

So I say,
"Five."

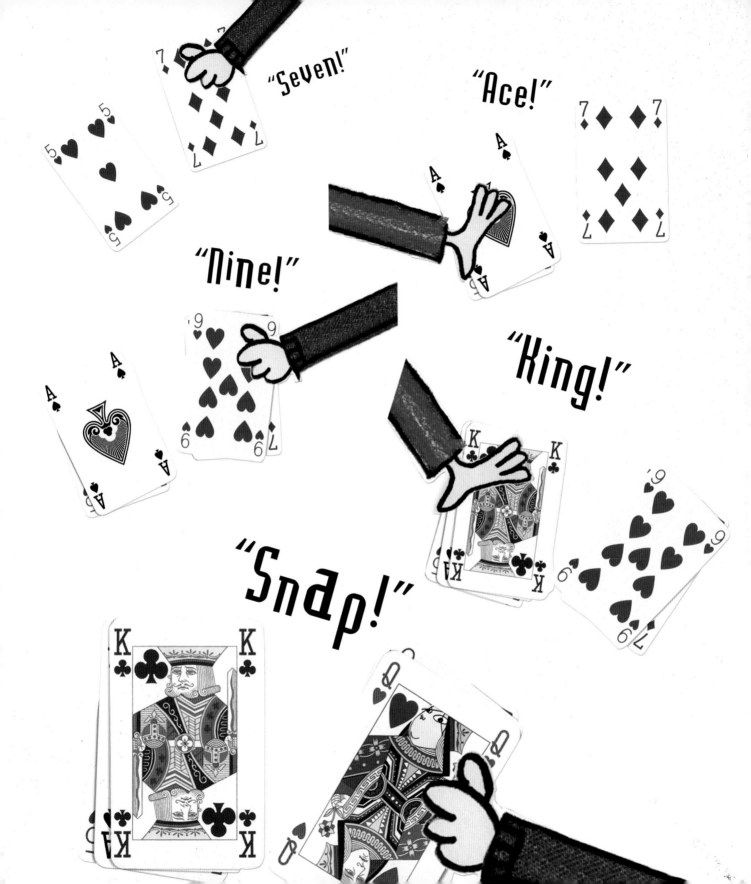

So then I say,
"How about a game of **snakes and ladders**?
You go
up the **ladders**
and
down the **snakes!**
The one who gets to
the **top** is the **winner!**
Do you understand?"

Lola says, "I **do** understand, yes, Charlie!"

I roll first and I shout...

"Six!

1..2..3..4..5..6

and
up
the
ladder!"

Then it's Lola's turn and she shouts...
"One, two, three! Snake!"

I say,
"Lola, what are you doing?
Snakes are for sliding down.
It's the rules!"

Lola says,

"Charlie, everyone knows snakes aren't all slippy and slidy.

They're easy to climb.

And...

I'm winning!"

Luckily I get another **six**,
which means **up** a **ladder!**

But Lola says,
     "Charlie! Dad says you are
not allowed to **climb** a **ladder!**
Not until you are **twenty-three!**"

     I say,
"Sorry. **Up** the **ladders**
          and **down** the **snakes.**

That's the rules!"

So Lola shakes the dice and says, "**four**!

1...2...3...4

snake!"

I say, "Bad luck. Now you've got to slide **down** all the way to the bottom.

I've won!"

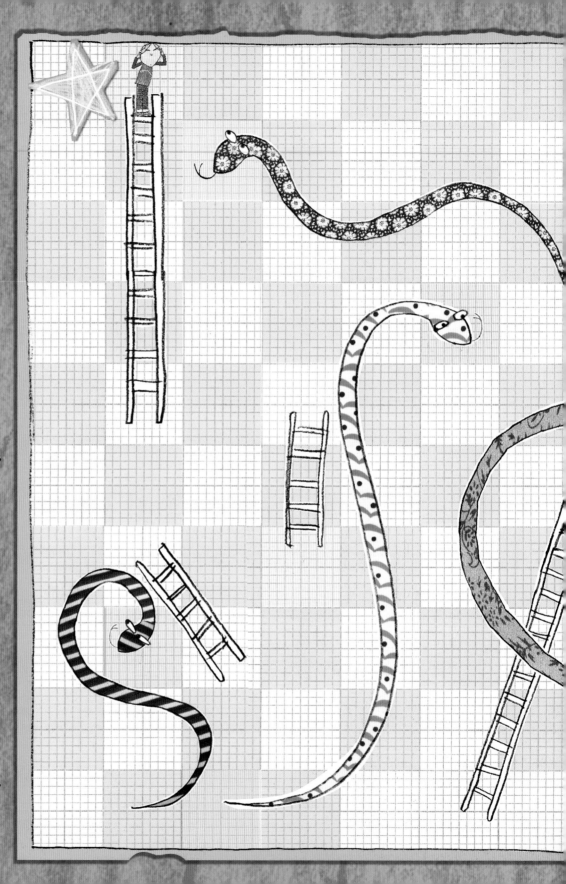

But guess what?
Lola pretends she's a **snake** charmer

and she charms the snake to the finish.

I say,
"But that's
cheating, Lola."

And she says,

"I've won!"

So I think of something
that Lola could
    never, never win!

When Dad takes us
        to the park I say,
"How about a **race**?
        It's **once** round
    the **bendy tree**!
Then **two** big swings
    on the **swing**!
Down the **slide**...
    and **first** one back
to the bench
    is
        the
            winner! OK?"

Lola says,
"But Charlie, I'm only little.
I haven't been on the big slide yet."

And I say,
"Well if you don't want
to win the race, Lola..."

But then Lola calls,
"Charlie!
Can
you
help
me?"

And even though
        I'm actually winning,
    I say,
"All right, Lola,
    I'm coming!
    Hold on."

We
w h o o s h
down
the slide
together.

Lola says,

"Wheeeee-eeee!
I'm winning!"

I say,

"Not for long!"

Then I say,
"And the
winner is...
me!

I've
won!

I've won!"

Then I remember Dad saying,
"Charlie, you must give Lola a chance,
because she's so small..."

And I say,
"Are you all right, Lola?"

And do you know what Lola says?
She says,

"That was fun!"

At bedtime, I say,
"Are you **asleep**
            yet, Lola?"

And Lola says,
        "Yes."

    So I say,
"How can you be **asleep**
if you are **talking** to me?"

She says,
        "I'm **sleep-talking!**"

    I say,
"The **first one** to
        fall **asleep** is
the **real winner!**"

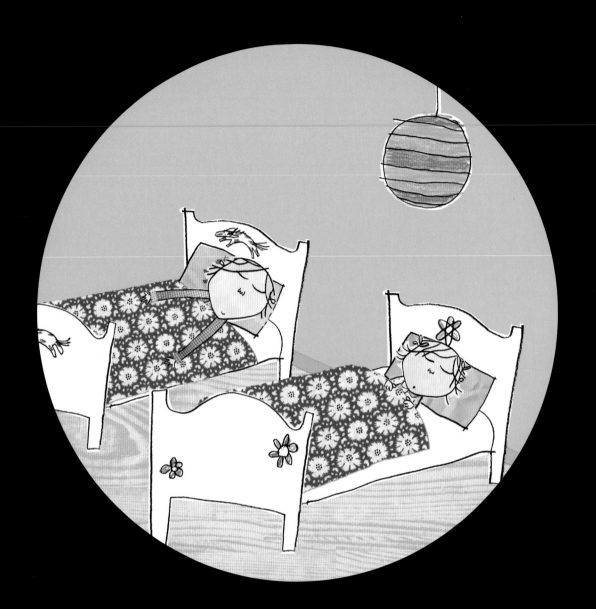

And then Lola whispers, "Charlie? I've won!"
And I say, "No... I've won!"
"I've won!"
"No... I've won!"
"I've won!"

I have this little sister Lola.
   She is small and very funny.
Today Lola is extremely excited
   because the man on the weather
says it's going to snow.

Lola cannot wait for the snow to come.

She says, "Snow is my favourite

and is my best."

I say, "Remember, Lola,

snow can only come when it is very, very cold.

Dad said it might not snow until midnight.

Or even tomorrow."

"I know,"
says Lola,
"but it is extremely
cold right now.
So I think the
snow will come
sooner rather
than midnight."

At bedtime, Lola says,
    "Do you think it has
started **snowing** now, Charlie?"

"No, go to sleep, Lola."

She says, "I can't because
          it might come while
I'm asleep, **sleeping**.

I'll just do **one more**
check...
          No snow.
       Not **yet**."

"See?" I say.
    "Go to sleep."

But a little bit later
    I hear Lola creeping
out of bed again.

"Ooooh!" she says.
"It's snowing!
    Charlie, come quick.
It's snowing, it's really,
        really snowing!"

So I watch the **snow** with Lola.
She says, "Can we **go out**
        and **play** in it **now?**"

"Not **now**, Lola," I say. "Wait until morning.
Then there'll be **more** and we can
go on the **sledge** with Marv and Sizzles.
And **you** can build a **snowman** if you want."

In the morning,
Lola shouts,

"Charlie!

Get up, Charlie!
Mum! Dad!

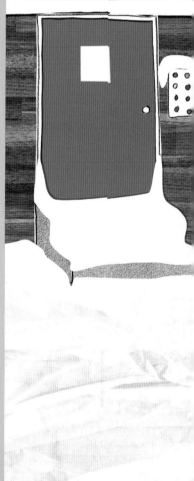

It's all gone
extremely white!"

So Mum and Dad took us to
the park and Lola was right,
everything had turned extremely,
completely white.

Then we see Marv and Lotta.
    And I say, "Where's Sizzles?"

"Yes," says Lola, "where's Sizzles?"

Marv points to a small pile of snow.
    "He's here!"
        he says. "Look!"

Lotta and Lola
make snow angels.

Lola says,
"Snow
is my
favourite
and my
best."

"I love **SnOw!**" says Lotta. "It's my **best** too."

Then we find a big hill and we all
go on the sledge. Even Sizzles!

I say, "Ready?
Steady?
Go!"

Wheeeeeeeee

eeeeee!

Then me and Marv
build a snowman.

Lotta says,
"Let's make a
snow doggy.
Come on, Lola!"

Later we go home to have some hot chocolate.
Marv says, "Mmmm. I love hot chocolate!"
Lola says,
"I love snow. Tomorrow I might put snowdog
and Sizzles on the sledge for a ride."

"I'm going to make a snow kennel," says Lotta,
"... and what about snow puppies?"

"Yes!" says Lola. "We can have lots of snow puppies!"

But when we go to the park the next day,
Lola can't make anything.

"It's gone!" she says.

"All the lovely snow is absolutely gone.
There's no more white, Charlie.
It's all cold
and wet
and brown.
And snowdog's gone."

So we go home again.

Lola says,
"Why can't we
         have **snow**
every day?"

And I say,
"Because it wouldn't be special.
Imagine you had a birthday
every day, so you had parties
and cakes and presents
all the time."

And Lola says,
"What's **wrong** with having
birthdays every day?"

And I say,
"It wouldn't be a treat, would it? I'm not sure you would like snow every day."

"I would, Charlie," says Lola. "Snow is my favourite and is my best."

Then I have a really good idea.
"Well, imagine a completely white land...

... where it's snowy and cold every day.
It's called the Arctic."

"Look at the polar bear," says Lola.
"What's he doing, Charlie?"
I say, "He's going for a swim."

"I'd like to go swimming," says Lola.
"Where's the beach?"
I say,
"There isn't a beach, Lola.
It's far too cold for us to go swimming."

Then I say, "And then there's this place right at the very bottom of the world, called the Antarctic, where you get seals and whales and....."

"Penguins!" says Lola.
"Don't the penguins look smart,
Charlie! They look like they're
going to a party!
I wish I was wearing my best, smartest
party dress, you know, the stripy one."

And I say,
"You couldn't wear your stripy dress in the Antarctic.
You have to wear your coat all the time
because it's so cold."

"Oh yes," says Lola, "I forgot."

Then I say, "But when it's all snowy, you can do this...

says, "but can we go home now?"

And I say, "But why? I thought snow was your favourite and was your best!"

Come on!"

And I say, "Isn't it amazing?"

"Wow!" says Lola.

And we slide on the ice with the penguins.

"Yes, Charlie," she

Lola says, "I do like it, Charlie. But I'm just a little chilly!"

"Snow is my favourite and my best, Charlie," says Lola, "but if it was snowy all the time there would be lots of things you couldn't do. So we're maybe lucky, we can do swimming and have stripy dresses and have snow.

But I do feel sad that the snow has all gone."

So I say, "I've got a

"A t^{ee}n_y weeny S_now^ma_n
            who lives in the fr^{ee}z^er!"
says Lola. "How did he
            get in there?"

"I don't know!" I say.

surprise for you.
        Don't look round!"

Lola says, "He's melting!"
I say, "Shall I put him back
in the freezer so we can keep him?"
"Oh no, Charlie," says Lola.
"Let's watch him melt!"

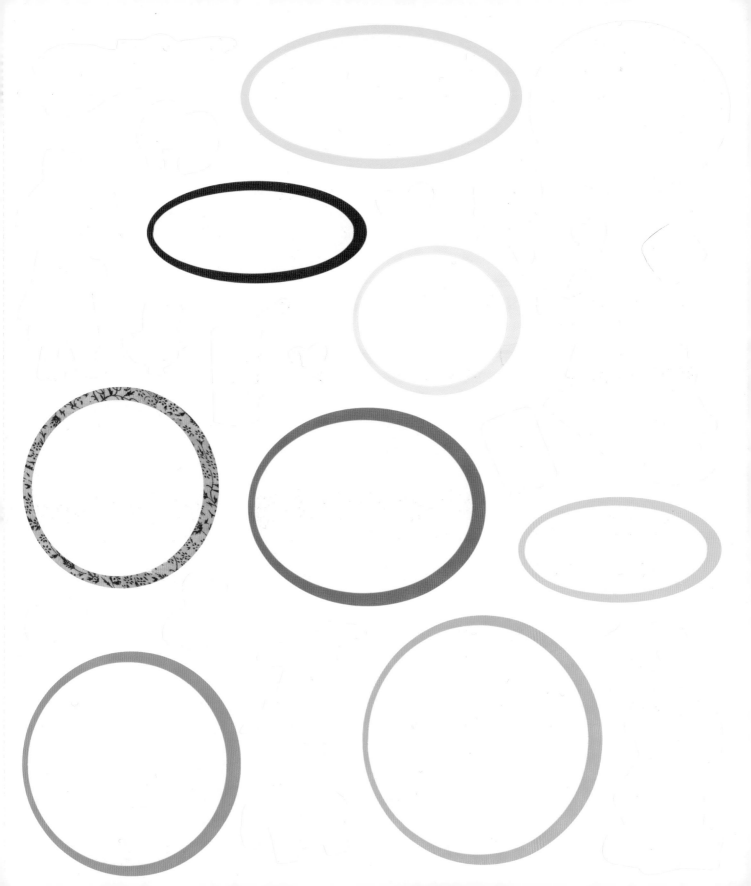